John Godfrey Saxe

The Fly-ing Dutchman

Or, the wrath of Herr Vonstoppelnoze

John Godfrey Saxe

The Fly-ing Dutchman
Or, the wrath of Herr Vonstoppelnoze

ISBN/EAN: 9783337309763

Printed in Europe, USA, Canada, Australia, Japan

Cover: Foto ©Andreas Hilbeck / pixelio.de

More available books at **www.hansebooks.com**

THE

FLY-ING DUTCHMAN;

OR,

THE WRATH

OF

Herr Vonstoppelnoze.

By JOHN G. SAXE.

WITH SIXTEEN COMIC ILLUSTRATIONS.

Tantæne animis *Teutonibus* iræ?

NEW YORK:

Carleton, Publisher, 413 Broadway.

(LATE RUDD & CARLETON.)

MDCCCLXII.

C. A. ALVORD,
ELECTROTYPER AND PRINTER.

CAP. X.

'T was an honest Dutchman,

Meinherr Vonstoppelnoze,

And ever, after dining,

He sat him down to doze,

And slept away the sultry day

In beautiful repose!

AND which it was an insect
    Come buzzing at his ear;
    But happy is the sleeper,
And nothing doth he fear,
Nor dream—unconscious mortal—
    An enemy is near!

CAP. XXX.

AND now the vile intruder
Hath sought the sleeper's head,
And there he marcheth gaily,
With bold and daring tread
But still the sleeper sleepeth
As he were of the dead!

HAT would the wicked insect?

What maketh he so sly?

Hath he a sting beneath his

wing,

That cursèd little fly?

Potstausend! cries the sleeper,

And openeth his eye!

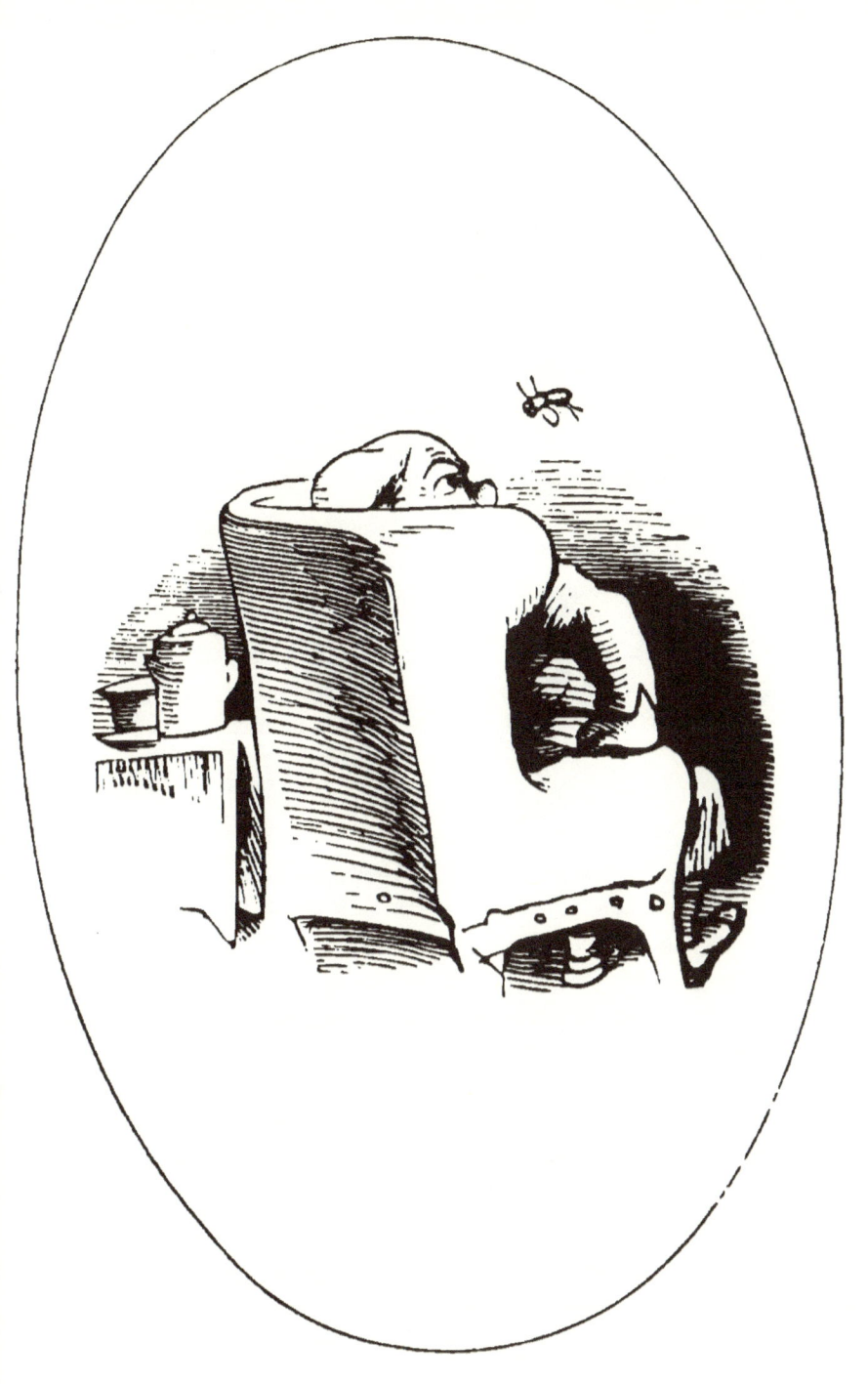

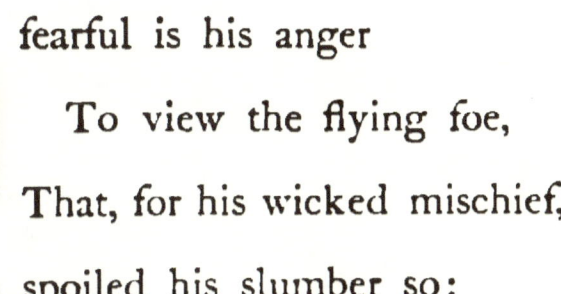fearful is his anger

　　To view the flying foe,

　　That, for his wicked mischief,

　　Hath spoiled his slumber so;

Sturmwetter! cries the Dutchman,

Ish dat der vay you go?

 ND now the wanton insect,

  All in a merry glee,

  (Was ever wight, by day or night,

So wondrous bold as he?)

Alights, for his refreshment,

  Upon a cup of tea!

CAP. VXX.

 _have him now!_ unto himself
Says Herr Vonstoppelnoze;
And, aiming at the enemy
The sturdiest of blows,
His fist goes flying through the air,
And—down the china goes!

H
E sees his broken crockery,

And heaves a heavy sigh;

There's slivers in his fingers,

There's fury in his eye;

But where—for he has vanished—

Has fled the wicked fly?

CAP. IX

AH! there he goes as large as life,

A-buzzing overhead;

That sturdy fist the mark has

missed,

And so the rogue has fled;

Mein Gott! cries Herr Vonstoppelnoze,

I thought the imp vas dead!

E makes a little flapper

    To flap the wicked fly;

    Ho! ho! says he, *we soon shall see—*

But now the imp is shy;

'Tis plain Meinherr Vonstoppelnoze

Can never flap so high!

AND so he mounts into his chair,

And flaps with might and main;

With such a swingeing blow as
that

The rascal must be slain;

Alas! the best of mortal plans

Full often prove in vain!

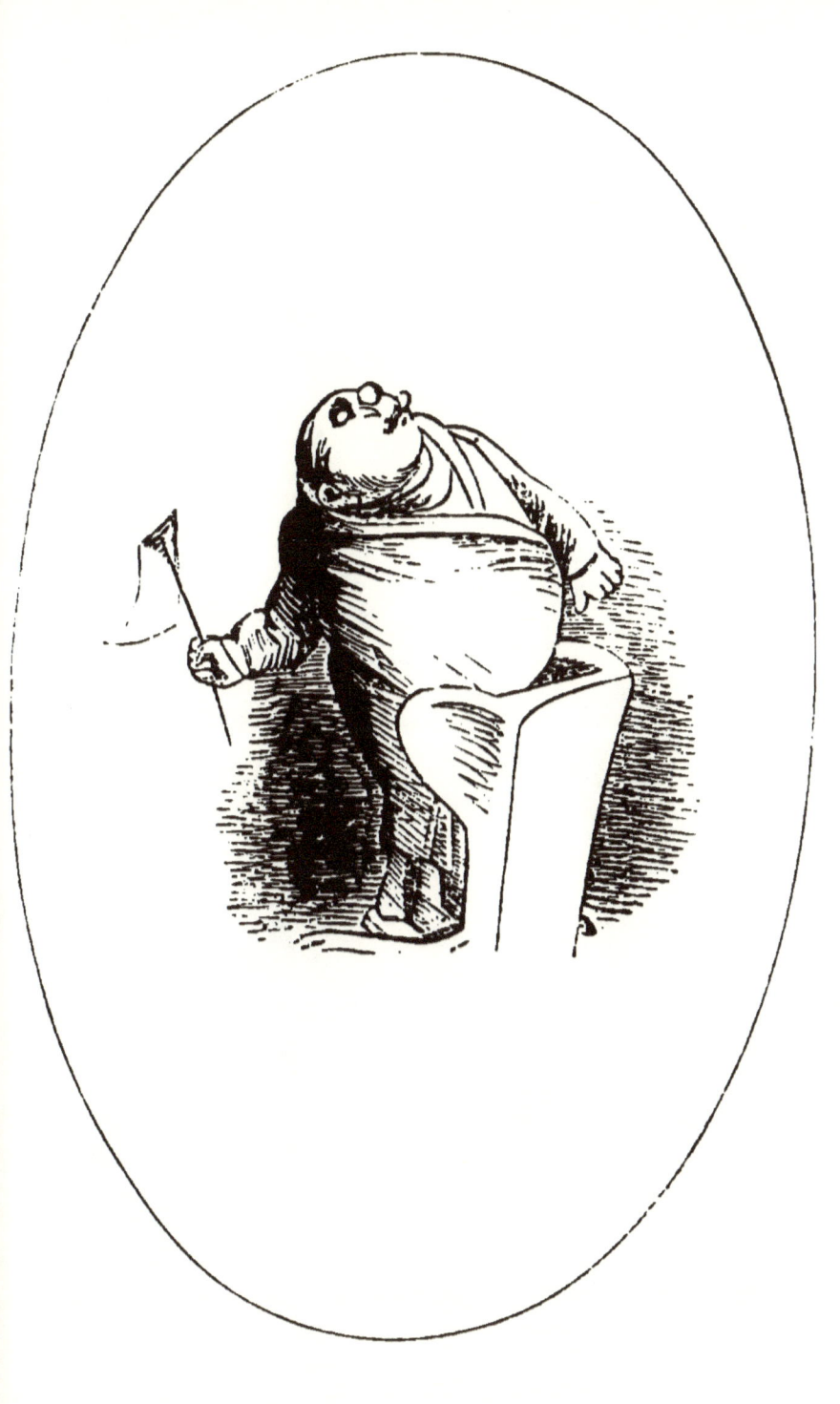

S O fierce a blow cannot be lost,

As you may well suppose;

Up flies the arm!—down falls

the chair!—

Away the insect goes—

And flat upon his chubby face

Comes Herr Vonstoppelnoze!

UT soon again with might
and main
He pounces on the foe;
His stick has caught a flower-pot,
And deals a deadly blow;
His time has come!—that hated fly
Will soon be lying low!

NOW there stands Herr Von-
  stoppelnoze,
 All in a merry glee,
Exulting o'er the fallen foe,
 And crying, *Now you see*,
You leedle tuyfel, vat you gets
Mit mettle-ing mit me!

ND now upon the vanquished fly

Behold the victor tread;

He tramples on his ugly limbs;

He tramples on his head,

Until the cursèd insect

A thousand times is dead!

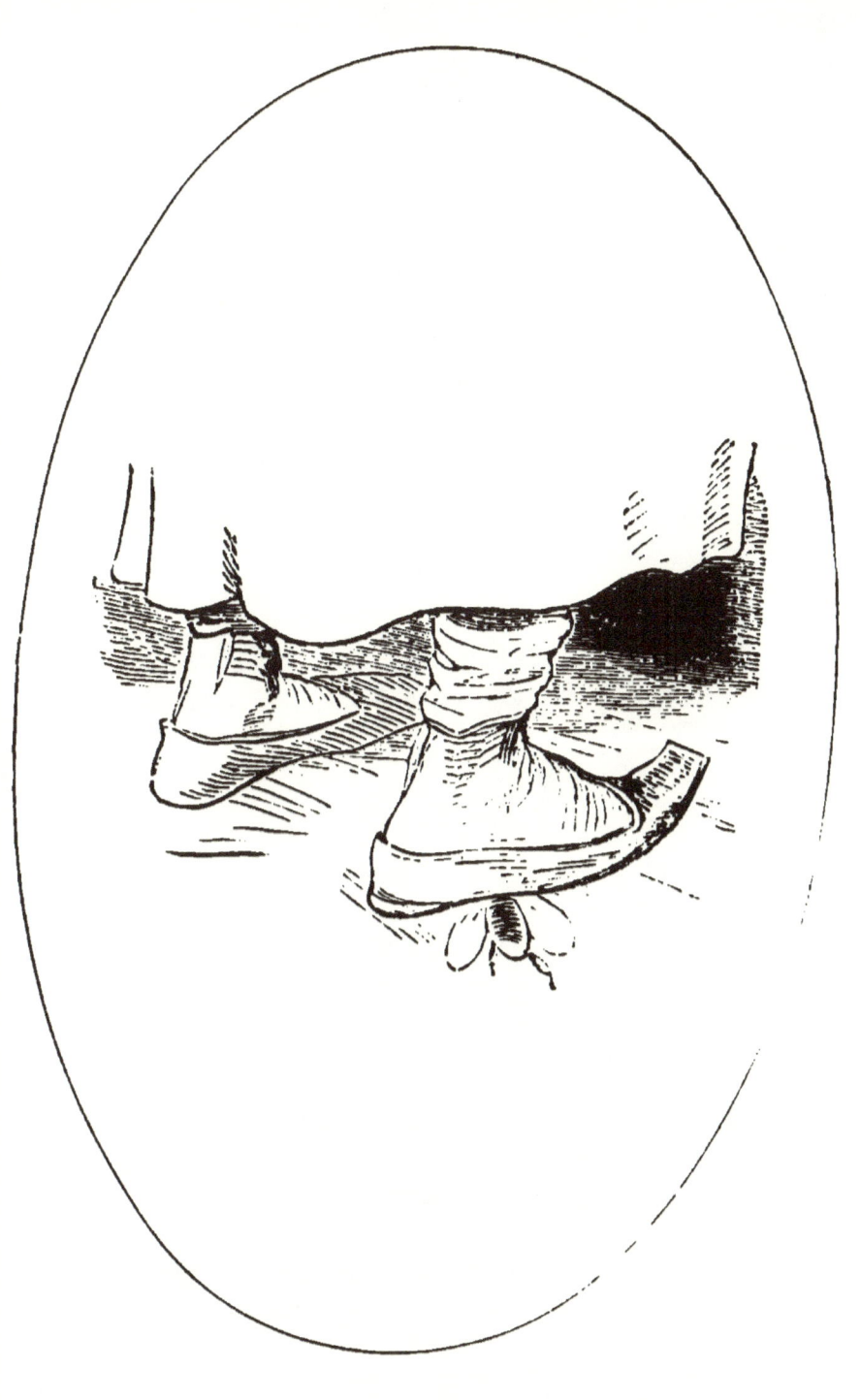

HE work is done!—the victor's joy

 Is tingling in his toes,

 So potently he can't refrain

From dancing as he goes;

Now I can go to shleep again!

 Says Herr Vonstoppelnoze.

NEW BOOKS

And New Editions Recently Issued by

CARLETON, PUBLISHER,

(LATE RUDD & CARLETON.)

413 *BROADWAY, NEW YORK.*

N.B.—The Publisher, upon receipt of the price in advance, will send any of the following Books, by mail, POSTAGE FREE, to any part of the United States. This convenient and very safe mode may be adopted when the neighboring Booksellers are not supplied with the desired work. State name and address in full.

The Cloister and the Hearth.
A magnificent new historical novel, by Charles Reade, author of "Peg Woffington," "Christie Johnstone," etc., etc., $1.25.

A Book about Doctors.
An amusing, entertaining, and gossipy volume about the medical profession—with many anecdotes. From English ed., $1.50.

Rutledge.
A powerful new American novel, by an unknown author, $1.25

The Sutherlands.
The new novel by the popular author of "Rutledge," $1.25.

The Habits of Good Society.
A hand-book for ladies and gentlemen. Best, wittiest, most entertaining work on taste and good manners ever printed $1.25.

The Great Tribulation.
Or, Things coming on the earth, by Rev. John Cumming, D.D., author "Apocalyptic Sketches," etc., two series, each $1.00.

The Great Preparation.
Or, Redemption draweth nigh, by Rev. John Cumming, D.D., author "The Great Tribulation," etc., two series, each $1.00.

Teach us to Pray.
A new devotional work on The Lord's Prayer, by Rev. John Cumming, D.D., author "The Great-Tribulation," etc., $1.00

Love (L'Amour).
A remarkable and celebrated volume on Love, translated from the French of M. J. Michelet, by Dr. J. W. Palmer, $1.00.

Woman (La Femme).
A continuation of " Love (L'Amour)," by same author, $1.00.

The Sea (La Mer).
New work by Michelet, author " Love" and " Woman," $1.00.

The Moral History of Women.
Companion to Michelet's " L'Amour," from the French, $1.00.

Mother Goose for Grown Folks.
A *brochure* of humorous and satirical rhymes for old folks, based upon the famous " Mother Goose Melodies," illustrated, 75 cts.

The Adventures of Verdant Green.
A rollicking humorous novel of English College life and experiences at Oxford University, with nearly 200 illus., $1.00.

The Old Merchants of New York.
Being entertaining reminiscences and recollections of ancient mercantile New York City, by " Walter Barrett, clerk," $1.50.

The Culprit Fay.
Joseph Rodman Drake's faery poem, elegantly printed,   50 cts.

Doctor Antonio.
One of the very best love-tales of Italian life ever published, by G. Ruffini, author of " Lorenzo Benoni," etc., etc., $1.25.

Lavinia.
A new love-story, by the author of " Doctor Antonio," $1.25.

Dear Experience.
An amusing Parisian novel, by author " Doctor Antonio," $1.00.

The Life of Alexander Von Humboldt.
A new and popular biography of this *savant*, including his travels and labors, with an introduction by Bayard Taylor, $1.25.

The Private Correspondence of Von Humboldt
With Varnhagen Von Ense and other European celebrities,$1.25.

Artemus Ward.
The best writings of this humorous author—illustrations, $1.00.

Beatrice Cenci.
An historical novel by F. D. Guerrazzi, from the Italian, $1.25

Isabella Orsini.
An historical novel by the author of " Beatrice Cenci," $1.25.

The Spirit of Hebrew Poetry.
A new theological work by Isaac Taylor, author " History of Enthusiasm," etc.—introduction by Wm. Adams D.D., $2.00.

Cesar Birotteau.
The first of a series of selections from the best French novels of Honore de Balzac. Translated from the latest Paris editions by O. W. Wight and Frank B. Goodrich (" Dick Tinto"), $1.00.

Petty Annoyances of Married Life.
The second of the series of Balzac's best French novels, $1.00

The Alchemist.
The third of the series of Balzac's best French novels, $1.00.

Eugenie Grandet.
The fourth of the series of Balzac's best French novels, $1.00.

The National School for the Soldier.
An elementary work for the soldier ; teaching by questions and answers, thorough military tactics, by Capt. Van Ness, 50 cts.

The Partisan Leader.
The notorious Disunion novel, published at the South many years ago—then suppressed—now reprinted, 2 vols. in 1, $1.00.

A Woman's thoughts about Women.
A new and one of her best works, by Miss Mulock, author of " John Halifax, Gentleman," " A Life for a Life," etc., $1.00.

Ballad of Babie Bell.
Together with other poems by Thomas Bailey Aldrich, 75 cts.

The Course of True Love
Never did run smooth, a poem by Thomas B. Aldrich, 50 cts.

Poems of a Year.
By Thomas B. Aldrich, author of " Babie Bell," &c., 75 cts.

Curiosities of Natural History.
An entertaining and gossiping volume on beasts, birds, and fishes, by F. T. Buckland ; two series, ea. sold separately, $1.25.

The Diamond Wedding.
And other miscellaneous poems, by Edmund C. Stedman, 75 cts.

The Prince's Ball.
A satirical poem by E. C. Stedman, with illustrations, 50 cts.

A Life of Hugh Miller.
Author of " Testimony of the Rocks," &c., new edition, $1.25.

Eric; or, Little by Little.
A capital tale of English school-life, by F. W. Farrar, $1.00.

Lola Montez.
Her lectures and autobiography, steel portrait, new ed., $1.25.

John Doe and Richard Roe.
A novel of New York city life, by Edward S. Gould, $1.00

LES MISÉRABLES.

(ADVERTISEMENT.)

THIS remarkable portraiture of society of the nineteenth century, to which Victor Hugo has given the richest twenty-five years of his life, is divided into five distinct novels, under the general title of LES MISÉRABLES. Each novel is complete. They will be published and sold separately in uniform binding.

They are entitled :—

I.
FANTINE.

II.
COSETTE.

III.
MARIUS.

IV.
IDYL OF THE RUE PLUMET
AND
EPIC OF THE RUE SAINT-DÉNIS.

V.
JEAN VALJEAN.

———

The price of the original French edition is $3 00 for each novel, in paper, while the American translation is 50 cents, in paper covers, and $1 00 in cloth binding.

———

₄ The Publisher will send any one of these novels by mail, postage paid, *on receipt* of price.